The Surprise On The Patio

Written and illustrated by Carlene Brod

To
Sophie
Happy Reading
Carlene Brod

To order additional copies of this book, contact:
Xlibris Corporation
1-888-795-4274
www.Xlibris.com
Orders@Xlibris.com

Thanks to Madison Brod, Harold Brog, and Marcia Brod for their helpful input into the book.

A beautiful plant with red shiny leaves sat on the patio.

The plant was watered every day by Maddie.

Happy Reading
Carlene Brod

One day a gray bird came to sit on the plant.
She sat there for days and days.
Maddie said to herself, "I think I will call this bird
Lovey Dove."

When Maddie came to water the plant
she found a surprise.

Maddie found sticks and twigs on top of the brown dirt.
This looked like a little nest.

Lovey Dove was sitting in the nest.

There were two eggs under Lovey Dove.
Maddie jumped.

Every day she tiptoed over to the plant to watch the eggs.
Lovey Dove just sat and sat on them.

Maddie was filled with excitement.
What should she do? Should she touch it?
She ran quickly to tell her mother.

Maddie's mother called her over to the plant. "Just be patient and keep watching. Something special will happen."

After many days, Maddie tiptoed close to the plant.
To her surprise there were two little eyes
peering out from a tiny head.

There were soft gray feathers on the head.
Little by little, two tiny birds appeared.

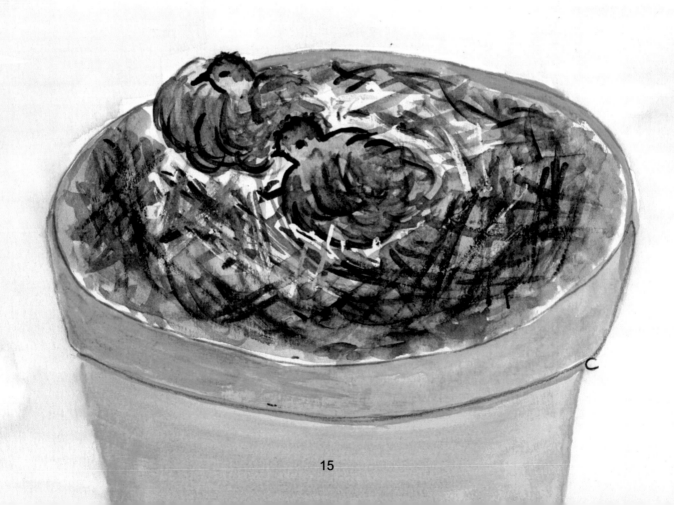

Lovey Dove stayed with them.
She sat there for days and days.

How did Lovey Dove get food for the baby birds?

17

One day a gray father bird came to sit on the fence next to the plant.

He brought food to Lovey Dove. Then he flew away.

One day when Maddie looked into the nest
Lovey Dove was gone. Where did she go?

She flew away to get food for the babies.
They were happy when the mother bird returned.

Each day the baby birds grew bigger and bigger.
One day the babies were jumping around
in the flower pot.

When would they fly?

Maddie went to look for the birds.
They were gone. Did they fly away?

They were not in the plant.
Maddie looked all around.

The birds were sitting together under the table on the patio.
Lovey Dove was gone.

"I guess the birds are getting ready to fly away," Maddie said to herself.

The next day only one bird was on the patio.

The other bird was gone.

Soon afterwards, the other bird was gone.
They flew far away.

The baby birds will grow up some day
and come back to lay new eggs.